boy shirt — buttons on <u>this</u> side

girl shirt — buttons on <u>that</u> side (don't ask me why!)

father sho[...]

↑ what are the little holes for? Feet air-conditioning?

father color — plaid

Amelia's
Family Ties

OR KNOTS?

shaving cream or clown makeup

knotty knot

by Marissa Moss

(and dutiful daughter? Amelia)

scrapbook for cozy family memories

American Girl™

↑ father slipper — no fuzz, <u>not</u> pink

If you're a man, it's called after-shave lotion. If you're a woman, it's called toilet water. (Yucch!) Whatever you call it, it stinks!

[...]er toilet — [...]he seat down!

moosaic cow

moovie star cow

This notebook is dedicated to
Judy,
who sent Amelia out into the world.

moosical
cow

Pleasant Company
Publications
8400 Fairway Place
Middleton, Wisconsin
53562

Book Design by Amelia

Library of Congress Cataloging-in-Publication Data
Moss, Marissa.
Amelia's Family Ties / by Marissa Moss.
p.   cm.

Summary: Ten-year-old Amelia takes her first solo journey,
to visit her father and his new family in Chicago.

ISBN 1-58485-079-5   ISBN 1-58485-078-7 (pbk.)

First Pleasant Company Publications printing, 2000

An   Amelia® Book
American Girl™ is a trademark of Pleasant Company.
Amelia® and the black-and-white notebook pattern
are trademarks of Marissa Moss.

Manufactured in Singapore

00 01 02 03 04 05 06 TWP   10 9 8 7 6 5 4 3 2 1

elevator
going down!

elevator going up!

mootant
cow

It looked like an ordinary letter. ↘

1863 Chickamauga #12C
Chicago, IL 60611

APRICOTS 7¢

flowers
26¢

TICK
TICK

Amelia
564 N. Homerest
Oopa, OR 97881

I'll be 90 years old before I spell this stupid word right!

It felt like a time bomb! ↗

   I love getting mail, even junk mail, but when I saw this letter I was almost afraid to open it. I could tell from the return address that it was from my dad. My dad — it's ~~wierd~~ ~~weird~~ ~~wierd~~ weird to even say that.

   I don't remember him at all. Cleo doesn't either, so she's no help, and Mom won't talk about him. At least she finally gave me his address so I could write to him. But that was months and months ago. I'd given up hope that he would write back, but he <u>did</u>!

Mom handed me the letter, but she didn't look happy about it. After all this time, she's still mad at him. ↘

What if the letter told me to BUG OFF!? ↓

What if he said he hated me and that's why he left in the first place? After all, right after I was born, he was gone. ↓

Cleo was really curious— she kept trying to stick her jelly roll nose in my letter.

Can I read it, too? C'mon, he's my dad, too.

No way! It's to me. Write your own letter to him if you want a letter back.

This is the ONLY thing I've *ever* gotten from my dad.

Dear Amelia,

I've written this letter a dozen times trying to think of the right thing to say, but I'm afraid there's no good excuse for not writing to you earlier. I meant to get a divorce from your mother, not from you and your sister. But I'm a journalist, and I began working in Japan after the divorce. I was there for ten years. From that distance, it seemed too difficult to stay in contact with a toddler (Cleo) and a baby (you).

Now I'm back in the United States, in Chicago. I've remarried and have a new family. You're a big sister now. Your baby brother George is six months old.

You have every reason to be angry with me, but now that you've found me, I'd like to stay found. I'd like to be part of your life. If you want to be part of mine, too, I hope you'll come spend a week with me this summer. You'll get to know me, my wife, Clara, and your half-brother. I've already talked to your mother, and she's agreed you can come. Think about it. I hope you decide to find out who your father really is.

Dad

Did I want to meet him? Of course I did! But I noticed he didn't sign the letter "Love, Dad," just "Dad." And being in Japan was a pretty lame excuse for not writing all this time. I know they have mail there because my pen pal, Mako, lives in Japan, and he writes me all the time.

I don't even know what it feels like to have a dad.

roll of the dad dice— which kind of dad will I get?

Mom was waiting for me to finish reading the letter. "Well," she asked, "do you want to go?"

I wanted to say yes and I wanted to say no, so I didn't say anything.

"Go where?" asked Cleo, the nosy one.

"Your father has invited both of you to visit sometime this summer," Mom said. "One at a time, so he can get to know you."

Other kids go to summer camp — I go to a new family.
At least I won't get a lot of bug bites.

Don't forget to pack your marshmallows!

HORSEBACK RIDING
SWIMMING
CAMP MEET-A-DAD
CANOEING
LANYARDS

Cleo couldn't <u>wait</u> to go, but he invited me first. I hated the idea that she might meet him before I did. →

I'm the oldest — I'll go first!

A Cleo-type dad would look like this.
↓

"I'll go," I said. "But I'm not going to like him. I'm just curious to see if he's anything like Cleo."

So it's settled. I'm going to fly on an airplane all by myself to a strange city (Chicago) to meet a strange man (my dad). The whole thing sounds **STRANGE!**

Cleo's jealous that I'm going to meet our dad first, so she's being extra mean.

If he <u>is</u> like Cleo, it will be TERRIBLE! He'll snore, chew with his mouth WIDE open, and get carsick—yucch!

You'll ruin my chance!

I should go first! If you go, he'll never want to see another kid as long as he lives!

TRA LA LA LA! I can't hear you! **TRA LA LA!**

I had to write my friend Nadia about it. →

Dear Nadia,
 Guess what? My dad finally wrote me back! I'm going to visit him in a couple of weeks. Do you have any advice about how to act around a dad? Are dads the same as moms? Mom says she's <u>nothing</u> like Dad, and that's one reason they're divorced. What if he's like a grown-up Cleo? **SCARY!**

luv, amelia
yours till the cake walks!

WAKE UP AND 20¢
SMELL THE COFFEE

Nadia Kurz
61 South St.
Barton, CA 91010

Hi!
I'm chocolate!

When she got my card, Nadia called, and after we talked, I felt much better.

C'mon, Amelia, I bet you've got a cool dad.

If he were really cool, he wouldn't have left.

Just give him a chance. And have fun — you'll be in a cool new city.

I'll try.

Carly's been great, too. But then, she has her own reasons for wanting me to meet my dad.

Carly has a whole list of questions for me to ask my dad. She's excited that he's a reporter, because that's what she wants to be.

Ask him where he went to school, how he got his first job, which newspaper he thinks is the best to work for, what's the difference between writing for magazines and newspapers, where he's trav...

But the question I want to ask is why? Why did he leave, and why did he stay away, and why doesn't he care about us?

At the airport, Cleo gave me a package to give our dad. She said if I dared to open it, she'd tear me apart. She looked like she meant it, too.

Cleo's gift for Dad — I don't even want to open it.

It's probably a stupid joke T-shirt like the one she gave Mom for Mother's Day.

BECAUSE I SAID SO!

Cleo's idea of a good Mom present

I gave Mom a hug, and then the flight attendant led me on the plane like I was a baby. I was excited about getting to fly all by myself, but a nosy lady sat next to me and she wouldn't stop talking. She wanted to know where I was going, who was going to meet me, if I was excited, and yakkity shmakkity. I told her I was an orphan going to meet a family that might want to adopt me, but three families had rejected me already, so I didn't expect them to like me. She looked at me like I was a hardened criminal and didn't say another word.

putting on lipstick

brushing teeth—
some people think
the plane is a
private bathroom

nightie-night!

peanut
guzzler

way too much soda!

privacy, please

the real hazard of air travel—
getting stuck and squashed behind
a snoring machine! There
go my knees!

Help! I'm
trapped!

zzzZZZZ

Fortunately, just when I thought I'd go crazy being
smushed on that plane, the pilot announced we'd be
on the ground in 10 minutes. HOORAY!

When the plane started to land, I started to
get nervous. What if this whole thing was a big
mistake? What if I went home with the wrong
person? Mom said Dad would have to sign for me
like I was some kind of special delivery. Surprise,
here's the package — me!

Before I could run and hide in the bathroom, the
flight attendant gave me some plastic wings and led
me off the plane to a man who was waiting there.

souvenir of my
u.M. flight →

cheapo, stick-on
← wings

I knew right away who he was — he had Cleo's nose!

He was kind of smiling, kind of not, like he was the one who was nervous.

He didn't look anything like me — so maybe he was just Cleo's dad, not mine.

He was carrying a teddy bear for me, like I was a baby or something.

I had tried to imagine his voice and face so many times. Now here he was — and he wasn't at all like I'd imagined. (Except he did have a head, two hands, and two feet.)

When he saw how big I was, he said he was sorry, but he didn't know what ten-year-olds were like. I said I didn't know what ten-year-olds were like either — I only knew what I was like.

I haven't seen anyone wear penny loafers since Mr. Nudel, my fourth-grade teacher. I hoped it was a good sign — I like Mr. Nudel a lot. Maybe my dad will be at least a little bit like my old teacher.

He did most of the talking. I couldn't think of what to say.

I didn't want to shake his hand, but I did. I noticed he had hair on his knuckles — GROSS! But I was polite and didn't say anything about it.

Dad kept asking questions — about Cleo and Mom, where we lived and where we went to school. I felt like yelling, "You'd know this stuff already if you cared about us!" He kept on talking like he was afraid of it being quiet. He talked about Chicago and pointed out famous places when we drove past them. He talked about his wife, Clara, who's a veterinarian, and about baby George and how smart and cute he was. (I felt very <u>un</u>-smart and <u>un</u>-cute.)

Chicago is a BIG city with lots of TALL buildings, but we drove into a neighborhood with beautiful old houses. (You could still see the skyscrapers.)

cup of cow-fee →

Of all the things my dad pointed out, my favorite was the cows. They weren't real, but sculptures, all painted and decorated differently, all over the city. They're part of a special outdoor art exhibit called "Chi-Cow-Go." (Chi-cow-go – Chicago – very funny!)

midnight cowboy ↓

I thought it would be so cool to live in one of those old houses, but Dad parked in the garage of the ugliest concrete box I'd ever seen.

cowsmonaut

↑ 100% cowton

↑ nice, cozy old house (It took forever to draw this, but it was the closest I could come to getting such a nice home.)

booooring modern apartment building (at least it has a view of the pretty hou...

cowabunga

I got out of the car. I still didn' feel like his daughter. And he didn't feel like a dad to me, exc I didn't know what that would feel like.

← cowsonants

cowtinents ↓

← cownfusion

President Lincown

cowstle →

cowliflower →

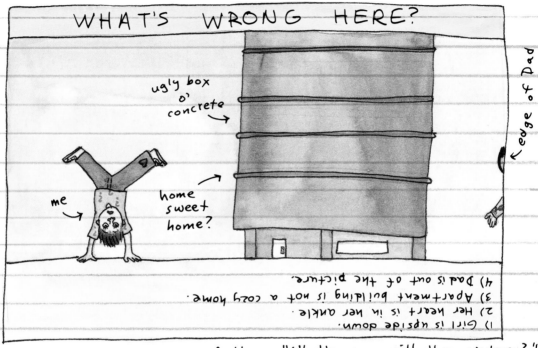

I felt pulled inside out and upside down because nothing was the way it was supposed to be.
↓

WHAT'S WRONG HERE?

ugly box o' concrete →

me →

home sweet home?

←edge of Dad

1) Girl is upside down.
2) Her heart is in her ankle.
3) Apartment building is not a cozy home.
4) Dad is out of the picture.

↳ It was like I was in one of those "What's wrong with this picture?" games from some magazine.

But I didn't have time to figure out what was wrong, because the door opened and things just got _more_ strange.

This woman with a too-big smile with too many teeth opened the door and started gushing. →

Everything she said ended in an exclamation point — it was all too much.

Ooooh! Amelia! We're SO excited to have you here! Your father has been SO eager to see how you've grown! You're just _a_-dorable! Isn't she a-dorable, Quentin? Come on, come on in! You must be starving!

What-in-cownation!

excowmation points

step-cow

shop cow

That was Clara. Technically, she's my stepmother, but I definitely wouldn't call her Mom. I just stood there, so Dad nudged me into the apartment.

"Welcome home, Amelia," he said. (At least he didn't talk in exclamation points.) "Let's go meet your brother." Half-brother, I said to myself, but I followed Dad into a room crammed with teddy bears. (Dad added my bear to the pile, I noticed.)

George was asleep in his crib, and I had to admit, he was very cute. Thank goodness he doesn't have a jelly roll nose.

It's o.k. George, you can have my bear.

I couldn't help it, I fell in love with George right away. I stroked his soft cheek gently with my finger.

"Hey, little brother," I whispered. "It's me, Amelia, your sister." He opened his eyes, looked right at me, and smiled. He grabbed my finger, and for the first time today, something felt right.

George's hand is so tiny, my finger looked like a giant's next to his.

Clara said I could hold George after she changed his diaper, so while I was waiting, I gave Dad the present from Cleo. (See, Cleo, I didn't open it, not even for a peek!)

It was a scrapbook Cleo had made all about herself — what a horror story!

For me? How sweet!

I could tell he really liked her present.

Cleo had put in old photos, ribbons, report cards, certificates, and other stuff so Dad would feel like he knew her.

Ooh, how cute — baby Cleo doing what comes naturally!

Cleo trick-or-treating at age four

an introduction to Cleo's tastes and eating habits

~ CLEO ~ can now swim, float, and kick

← swimming certificate

lanyard from summer camp

FOR EXCELLENCE IN SCIENCE
Cleo
SCHOOL SCIENCE FAIR

science fair certificate ↑

second grade spelling bee award

Dad smiled and said I have an amazing sister. Great! He already likes Cleo better than me. Well, I don't care, because I don't like _him_.

I said I was tired and went to my room. I felt like crying. What had I expected, anyway? What did I _want_?

I'm sleeping in the guest room. It's Dad's office when he works at home, but there's a fold-out couch, too. ↘

It was a nice room, better than I thought from the outside, but I couldn't get comfortable.

I dreamed I baked up a new family, only instead of people, I got a cake. When I woke up, I was still here, with Dad, Clara, and George, but I did smell cake — pancakes! That was a good way to start the day.

After breakfast, we went to the zoo. I thought it would be fun, but it seemed as if I was behind bars being watched all the time, the most strange animal of them all. Dad and Clara looked at me as though I were about to explode — and they asked the stupidest questions ever.

I tried to imagine we were a normal family, like all the other families at the zoo. But I didn't feel normal. And I didn't feel like this was my family.

So, do you like your school, Amelia? How's your house?

Do you play soccer?

Gabool!

Did you have a good teacher?

What's your favorite subject in school?

<u>My</u> question is, "Why do grown-ups ask so many questions?" What if I asked them, "Do you like your work? Do you have a good boss? Do you play soccer? What's <u>your</u> favorite breakfast cereal?" What I really wanted to ask was, "Why did you leave, Dad?" and "Is it true you picked the name Amelia? Why? Do I mean <u>anything</u> to you?" But I'm too scared to ask <u>those</u> questions.

rub-a-dub-dub a George in a tub

The best part of the day was giving George his bath. He laughed when I played games with him, and he has the most beautiful smile. I didn't know it would be so much fun to be a big sister. Cleo always complains about it. But then she's not very good at it. I can tell that George thinks I'm a <u>perfect</u> sister.

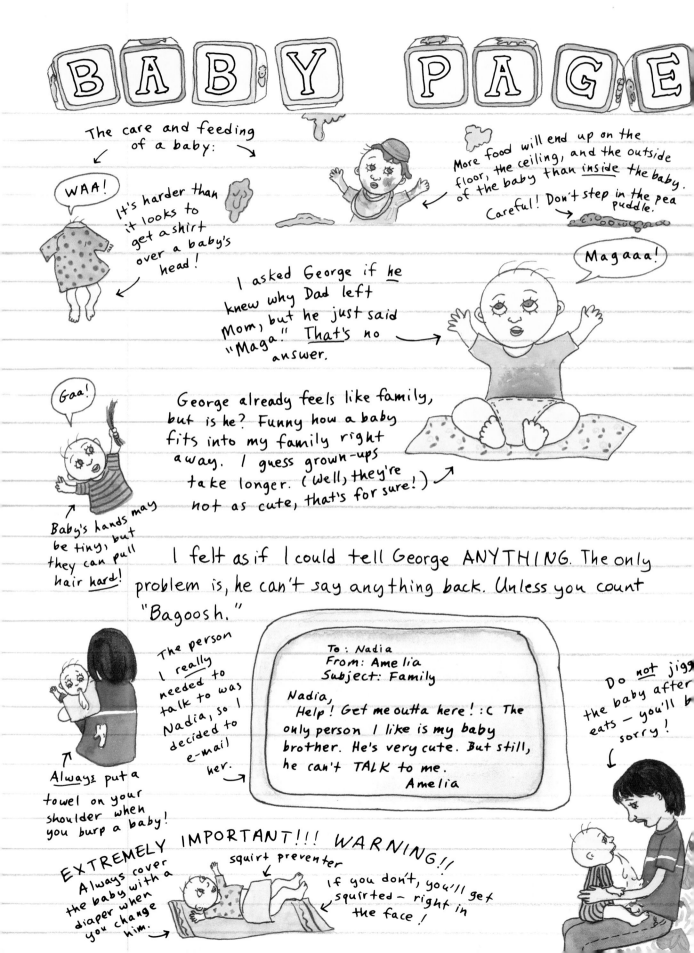

Clara collects these miniature shoes — what's that about? Mom would NEVER have → these!
↓

Zebra shoe

Cinderella slipper

GOING BUGGY 7¢ 7¢

↑ polka dot heel

Aladdin slipper ↑

platform tennis shoe (now that makes sense!) ↑

Clara's really bugging me. She's NOT like Mom at all. Clara always stands too close when she talks to me, and she's constantly touching me — on the arm, the shoulder, the hand — as if she's afraid I'm really a ghost.

BOOO!

Ooooh, scary! ↓

At least Dad's getting better at talking to me in a normal way. Today was actually kind of fun because just the two of us went to Navy Pier. The best part was the giant Ferris wheel.

checkerboard shoe ↑

I could tell Dad was having fun, too, not just doing a dad-job like at the zoo.

Even from the top, I couldn't see the other side of Lake Michigan. That's one BIG lake!

↑ striped wedgie

↑ powder puff high heel

pointy sharp shoe

disco dance shoe (don't trip!)

one BIG Ferris wheel

This candy looks good, but → tastes terrible.

← watermelon ribbon

licorice sandwich

syru
a u
b

Then we went to a GREAT candy store, and I got to pick out a ton of candy. Grown-ups only let you do stuff like that when they feel guilty. That's fine with me — I can eat the candy without feeling sweet about the person who bought it.

gummy penguin →

The BEST part of all was when I got back to the apartment. I checked my e-mail and there was a message from Nadia! Now I don't feel so alone.

To eat or not to eat, that is the quest

Too swee
not too
that i
que

gummy gums (and teeth!) →

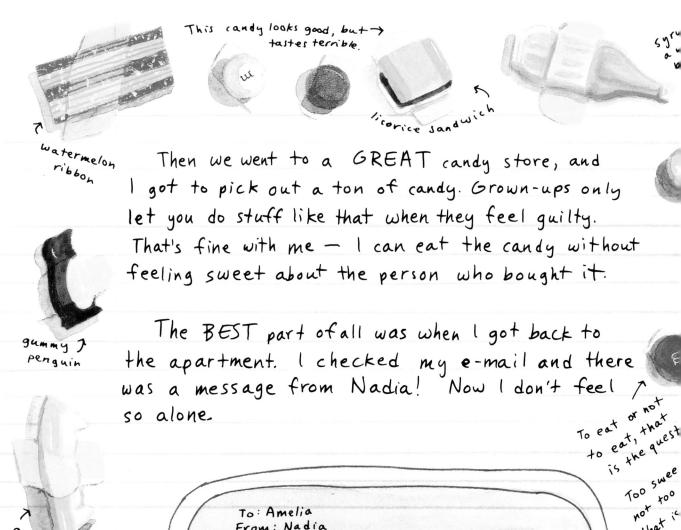

To: Amelia
From: Nadia
Subject: Family Ties

Amelia,
    Give your dad and stepmom a chance. After all, you only just met them. It takes a while to get to know someone. Remember how shy I was with you at first? I bet things will get better (and if they don't, think of it as a vacation from Cleo). :)
                                    Nadia

Maybe Nadia's right. Every day things get a little easier. Maybe we're all getting used to each other. Even Clara wasn't as annoying tonight.

← candy to build with →

still life with cow →

abstract art cow →

Cowna Lisa — note the mysterious smile →

 Or should I say the "Moona Lisa?"

classical cow ↓

Today we all went to the Art Institute. There were lots of famous paintings, but my favorites were these cool boxes by an artist named Joseph Cornell. George liked them best, too.

Some were windows to a landscape. ↓

They were little worlds wrapped in a box, kind of like dream packages.

Some boxes had mirrors so you could see both sides of the things in the box at once.

If I made a box of _my_ world right now, it would look like this. ↓

bicycle on a wire — what a balancing act! →

Mama Bear for my mom

notebook paper ↓

Japanese luck god for Mako

jump rope for Carly

pencil for Nadia ↘

pen for Leah

baby doll — George is already part of my world

realistic cow

nail polish for Cleo

notebook cover pattern for the floor

shoe for Clara and newspaper for Dad — outside of the box

collage cow ↓

But my world's too much of a mess right now to fit neatly into ANY box. Maybe writing a story will help. Words can hold a _lot_ of stuff. Anyway, writing always makes me feel better.

I look at George, who is <u>so</u> adorable, and I think I must have been that cute when I was a baby. Why didn't my da adore <u>me</u>?

a story →

The Orphan

← starting here

Once there was a boy who didn't have any parents. And he was happy that way. He lived by himself in a little house, and he could eat pizza for breakfast and not make his bed, and no one would nag him about it.

But one day a man and a woman came to his house. "Oh, you poor thing," they said. "You must be so sad and lonely. How would you like it if <u>we</u> lived with you and took care of you, and you could call us Mom and Dad?"

Call me Mom.

Call me Dad.

← nicey-nice lady

nicey-nice man →

The boy <u>didn't</u> like it, but he didn't know what to say. The man and the woman didn't wait for an answer anyway. They barged right in and started acting like parents.

"Go clean your room," said the dad.

"And then we'll have some nice brussels sprouts and liver for dinner," said the mom.

a deadly combination! →

← two horrible smells, two terrible tastes in one awful meal!

The boy went to his room, but he didn't clean it. There was only one thing to do. He packed a suitcase with all his favorite stuff, climbed out the window, and ran away.

He found a new little house, even nicer than the first one, and he lived happily ever after.

It happened! Worse than a mountain of brussels sprouts! Worse than making a million beds! Just when I thought MAYBE things were getting better, things got WAY, WAY WORSE!

RED ALERT!

I've been mad at my mom. I've been mad at Leah. I've been mad at Cleo. But I've _never_ been as mad at anyone as I am at Clara.

SHE READ MY NOTEBOOK!

I couldn't believe it! At dinner, she turned to me and said "So, you're a writer, like your dad. You're really good."
I asked her what she meant. And she said, "Well, I saw that story in your notebook—"

ENEMY INVASION! CONTAMINATION HAS OCCURRED!

I EXPLODED!

All the stuff I'd kept inside came pouring out.
"HOW COULD YOU?! THAT'S PRIVATE!!
HOW WOULD YOU LIKE IT IF I READ <u>YOUR</u>
DIARY OR <u>YOUR</u> LETTERS?!

I HATE YOU!"

I ran into my room and SLAMMED the door.
I was so ANGRY I didn't know what to do, but I knew
I couldn't stay in that apartment one minute longer.
I started packing my suitcase. Maybe I could get an earlier
flight home. If I couldn't, I'd just live at the airport until
it was time to go.

all the comforts of home

I could live off of
extra packages of pretzels
and peanuts from the
airplanes.

My suitcase could be
a cozy tent to sleep in.

The hot air blower in the
bathroom could massage
my back.

First thing I did was to decontaminate my notebook.

It took 17 tissues to wipe every page.

when I finished packing, I just huddled on the sofa, looking out the window. Why was everything turning out so bad? From this ugly concrete building to this ugly concrete lump in my stomach.

Are better lives happening just across street? Do people in pretty houses lead pretty lives?

I just <u>had</u> to talk to someone, so I called Nadia. I told her what had happened and that I was packed and ready to go.

"But Amelia," Nadia said, "you don't have to like Clara, just put up with her. How are things with your dad? That's the main question."

I told her the main question wasn't answered yet. Maybe it never would be. When Nadia heard that, she said I should definitely stick it out. "You've got to get to know your father better, and he has to learn who <u>you</u> are." She's right. Nadia usually is.

Even though I couldn't see Nadia, her voice made me feel she was right there with me.

I thought Dad would see my suitcase ready to go and be so glad to get rid of me, he'd drive me → to the airport right away.

Dad knocked quietly on the door and came in. I thought he'd yell at me for yelling at Clara, but he didn't. He looked very sad.

   "I'm sorry, Amelia," he said. (It seems like he's always apologizing to me.) "What Clara did was wrong. I'm shocked she read your notebook, but I promise you — she promises you — it won't happen again. She didn't understand how important your notebook is to you, but I do." He smiled a little. "Because I kept one, too, when I was your age."

That was a surprise. Part of me was still mad, but part of me wondered what kind of notebook he had and did he still have it? Did he like to draw the way I do? Would I ever get to see his notebook? Are boys' notebooks different from girls'?

comic notebook ↙

science notebook ↓

regular notebook ↗

sports notebook →

It's funny, but knowing about his notebook made me feel like he really is my father. Cleo may have his nose, but I have his writing.

   "You're packed," Dad said, looking at my suitcase.
   I still didn't say anything.
   Dad kneeled in front of me and took my hands. They may have been hairy, but his hands felt warm and strong. I didn't want him to let go.

My little hand in his big one was like George's tiny fingers in mine. →

"Listen, Amelia," he said, "I know I've been a terrible father, and I keep saying and doing the wrong things, but I AM trying. Please stay."

He even had tears in his eyes! I didn't know dads could cry. I wanted to hug him, but I couldn't. All I could do was nod my head.

For a minute I thought <u>he</u> was going to hug <u>me</u>. But he didn't. He patted my head softly instead.

"Thank you," he said, and he left.

After he was gone, the room felt thick and cottony with quiet. I was mo alone than ever.

I didn't want to cry, but I could feel the tears in my eyes. Maybe what he said should have been enough, but it wasn't. I lay in bed and cried until I fell asleep.

My heart feels all broken to pieces, but I can't say why.

what do I want from him, anyway? What do I expect?

Usually writing things down helps me figure them out, but not today.

I can't draw what's wrong, either — I don't know <u>what</u> to draw.

It all looks normal, but <u>nothing's</u> the same anymore. →

Simple spoon →

regular old bowl ↑

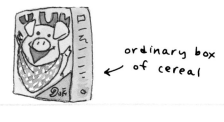

ordinary box ← of cereal

It was hard to get up and act like everything was normal this morning. Clara said how sorry she was, but then she acted like she didn't want to be around me. She rushed off to work, leaving Dad, George, and me alone, which was fine by me.

DANGER! bomb about to EXPLODE! ↑ Amelia

Dad tried to be all jokey as he ate oatmeal, pretending to be Papa Bear. ↑

George was the only one who acted the way he always does, smearing cereal up his nose and in his ears. ↓

It looks like cereal, but acts like face cream. ↑

Then Dad had to go to work in his office — that is, in my bedroom. He said he had an important phone interview and asked me to watch George. I'd never taken care of a baby all by myself, but I didn't think it'd be hard.

handful of mush →

My first job was to wash off all the dried-on cereal - yucch! ←

what's the point of the bib? Oatmeal still goes EVERYWHERE! →

food or toy? ←

And at first, it wasn't. I read George a book, and we played with his toys. Then suddenly he erupted, like a science-fair volcano!

← George crying — loudest of all!

bomb exploding

red, red face →

big, open WAILING mouth

Babies' faces crumple up when they cry.

I tried EVERYTHING! I made silly faces, I made begging faces, I made *desperate* faces. PLEASE, George, tell me what you want! I can't read your mind!

I brought him:

airplane taking off

his pacifier

his rattle

a teddy bear

a teething cookie — BABY-O

a book — GOOD DAY! KITTY KAT

a bottle

a washcloth (well, nothing else worked!) →

← rock concert

jackhammer

I was scared something was really wrong, but he couldn't tell me *what*. Then, just as I brought him my sock, he stopped! I'm not sure it was my sock that did it, but at least it was over.

George acted like nothing was wrong. "What was that all about?" I asked him. He *still* couldn't tell me why. →

↑ noise measurement

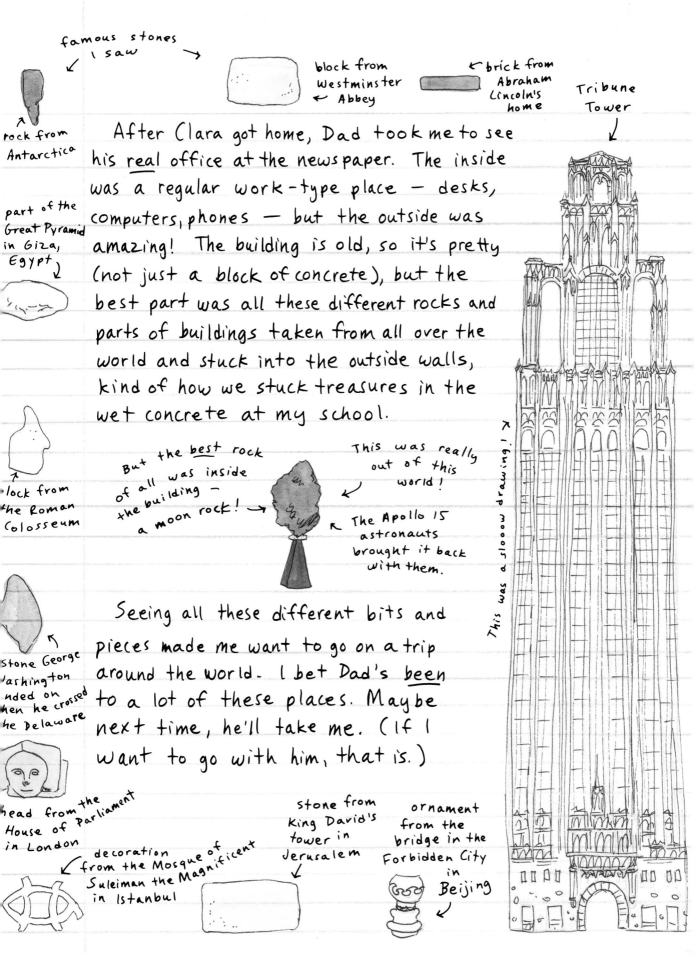

famous stones
I saw

rock from Antarctica

block from Westminster Abbey

brick from Abraham Lincoln's home

Tribune Tower

part of the Great Pyramid in Giza, Egypt

After Clara got home, Dad took me to see his real office at the newspaper. The inside was a regular work-type place — desks, computers, phones — but the outside was amazing! The building is old, so it's pretty (not just a block of concrete), but the best part was all these different rocks and parts of buildings taken from all over the world and stuck into the outside walls, kind of how we stuck treasures in the wet concrete at my school.

rock from the Roman Colosseum

But the best rock of all was inside the building — a moon rock!

This was really out of this world!

The Apollo 15 astronauts brought it back with them.

This was a slooow drawing!

Seeing all these different bits and pieces made me want to go on a trip around the world. I bet Dad's been to a lot of these places. Maybe next time, he'll take me. (If I want to go with him, that is.)

Stone George Washington landed on when he crossed the Delaware

head from the House of Parliament in London

decoration from the Mosque of Suleiman the Magnificent in Istanbul

stone from King David's tower in Jerusalem

ornament from the bridge in the Forbidden City in Beijing

This is my daughter, Amelia

↑
rock from "Injun Joe's" cave, Missouri (from Mark Twain's book)

Dad introduced me to everyone as his daughter and he didn't even seem embarrassed. →

↑
stone from the Alamo in Texas

↑
chip off the Berlin wall in Germany (when there was a Berlin wall)

↑
from the Arch of Triumph in Paris

It looked hard to write for a newspaper. You have to write fast, and you can't make up whatever you want to happen (like in my stories). I don't think I'll be that kind of writer when I grow up.

We went to a place called the morgue, only it wasn't full of dead people, just more computers, photo files, and old newspapers. Dad wanted to show me some articles he'd written. I have to admit, it was cool seeing his name in print like that. (But what I'd really like to read is one of his notebooks — with his permission, of course. I'm not a snoop like Clara!)

He gave me an article to keep from his "clip file" (no, not toenail clippings — newspaper clippings!).
↓

In Japan, Work Is Play

The politeness and civility of the Japanese is legendary. What's not so widely understood is how this affects the sense of community and common changes rub against the grain, but no more so than in older, more conservative sectors of populations in general. We, as

↑
stone from Independence Hall in Pennsylvania

decoration from the Cathedral of Notre Dame in Paris →

rock from → the Parthenon in Athens

ornament from the Santa Sophia in Istanbul →

I tried to remember all the questions Carly wanted me to ask about being a reporter, but I couldn't. Dad said he'd call Carly and talk to her himself. I'm glad <u>somebody's</u> getting something out of this visit.

In Japan he was a foreign correspondent, so he wrote about stuff that happened there. Now he writes for the editorial page.

Dad's desk →

↑ stone from the Great Wall of China

Seeing his office made me feel funny — like I was part of his life, but I wasn't. There were photos of Clara and George, but not of me and Cleo. Would he put some up now, add us to his family collection? He <u>still</u> didn't feel like my dad. I was getting bits and pieces of him, like the stones on the building, but it wasn't enough.

↑ rock from Bunker Hill, Massachusetts

Back at the apartment, I could tell Clara still didn't want to be around me. Dad could tell, too, because he put on a fake happy voice and said he'd been planning a special night for me — dinner out, just the two of us. I didn't care about dinner, but maybe he'd finally tell me what I wanted to know.

↑ tile from Forbidden City in Beijing

← cow from Roy's Steak House in Fresno (just kidding — I wanted to get a cow in)

stone from → St. Peter's Cathedral in Rome

stone from ↑ Tower of Tears in Amsterdam

The   Dinner

glow of candle light →

Fancy restaurants do not have:

toothpicks with frills on top

packets for mustard and ketchup

non-dairy creamer

french fries — instead they have *French Fried Potatoes*

The menu was like a heavy book, not the kind printed on a place mat that you're supposed to color on. ↓

The dinner was at a fancy-shmancy restaurant, the kind with cloth napkins and big thick menus with tassels on the ends. I know Dad was trying to be elegant and special, but a diner with a jukebox would have been more my style. There were so many forks, I wasn't sure which one to use. I was afraid I'd make some big embarrassing mistake.

usual kid menu with a maze, word search, and dot-to-dot →

I felt really small. The menu was bigger than my head!

Pretty nice, huh?

Uh, yeah.

Do they have plain pizza?

At least I got a drink with a little paper umbrella and a maraschino cherry.

I've always wanted one of these. ↓

Even the bread was served in a fancy way, with tongs, like something delicate or a jewel. →

More things fancy restaurants don't have: ↓

↑ wrapped-up crackers (or _any_ kind of crackers)

I ended up with plain spaghetti. (I don't even want to _know_ what foie gras or béchamel are. They sound GROSS — definitely _not_ edible.)

Dad talked about living in Japan and the things they eat there (worse than foie gras!) and how he missed it. But what I really wanted to know was why he left us.

↑ soda served in a can

Then I remembered how I felt when I was trying to cheer up George. How could I help him if he couldn't tell me what was wrong? And how could Dad know what _I_ needed if I didn't tell him? He couldn't read my mind. So finally I did it. I asked the question.

Dad, why did you and Mom get divorced? How come you left us?

Help! My elbow is glued to the table!

↑ sticky table-tops

There was a big silence. I was afraid he hadn't heard me, and I'd never get the nerve to ask again.

But he _had_ heard me. He put his fork down and took a deep breath.

↑ sugar packets with pictures of Hawaii on them

metal napkin holders ↙

plastic utensils — combination spoon and fork →

He looked sad. ↑

Amelia, I'll be honest with you—
it was a painful divorce. I needed
to travel and couldn't be with your
mother as much as she needed. We
fought about it for years. It had
nothing to do with you or your sister,
but after the divorce, your mother
and I didn't want to see each
other. The two of you were so
young, I thought it would be
easier if you never
knew me.

"Easier for who?" I wanted to know. "For us or for you?"

"I guess for both," Dad said. "But I was wrong. It was
a big mistake. I should never have left <u>you</u> just because
your mother and I couldn't get along. I'm <u>really</u> sorry."

Even if he <u>was</u> sorry, I still didn't feel better.
Something important hadn't been said yet. I wasn't
sure what it was, but I'd know it when I heard it.

we both just
sat and stared
at the napkins
in our laps for
a while. It was my turn to say <u>something</u>. I had to think of wh

"So," I said, "is it true you picked out my name?"

Dad smiled then. "Yes," he said, "I did. When
you were born you were so alert already, so eager
to be part of the world. I thought you would be a
great adventurer, someone willing to take chances,
someone like Amelia Earhart."

More things fancy restaurants have: →

Parsley as a decoration on plates (a green vegetable pretty? Are you crazy?!)

Pick me!

No, me!

desserts wheeled to your table on a cart, so you can <u>see</u> what you want to pick, not just read about it

Dad looked right into my eyes and then he said it, what I'd been waiting to hear all this time. "I loved you the minute I saw you."

waitpeople who say, "I'll be your server for tonight" instead of "whaddya want?"

I couldn't help it, I had to smile. →

I felt like a big weight was gone. ←

a separate menu just for drinks ↗

Suddenly that plain spaghetti tasted like the best spaghetti in the world. We both started eating and talking, and it all felt so perfect. <u>This</u> is what it's like to have a father, I thought. It wasn't hard at all.

Dad even told me baby stories about myself. ↓

Even when I was just a couple of months old, I liked to grab onto pens.

And I loved to stare at the ceiling — Dad thought I was turning cracks into pictures. I probably was, too.

Things got better after that. Even Clara! The next morning, she finally looked at me again and really talked to me.

She was being real, not fake-sweet.

she looked like she hadn't slept well in a long time.

I'm new at being a mother — and a stepmother, too. George is teaching me how to be a mom for him, but I don't know how to be a stepmom for a ten-year-old. You'll just have to show me.

will you forgive me?

I looked at George. He was sitting in his high chair grinning at me. I guess since Clara is George's mom, she can't be all bad.

"O.K.," I said, and I started to spoon applesauce into George's mouth.

Best of all, Dad handed me a package.

Not a teddy bear, not candy, not a joke T-shirt, but a . . .

. . . NEW NOTEBOOK! And a whole set of cool Japanese pens!

"I finally found the right present," Dad said. "I just had to find out who you were first."

He opened his arms, and I walked into the first Dad hug of my life.

I'm using my new pens to write a new story.

~ FAMILY LIFE ~

There was this girl who had three different families, all in the same apartment building. On the first floor lived her father and brother, on the second floor lived her mother and sister, on the third floor lived her grandma and grandpa. She ate breakfast with one family, lunch with another, and dinner with another. It was all very confusing.

So the girl had an idea. She sawed holes in the floors and ceilings and put in a long pole like they have in fire stations. Then she could slide from apartment to apartment easily and look up one hole and down another.

Hand me my notebook, please.

Oh no, I left my notebook upstairs! Or was it downstairs?

It was still hard work, going from home to home, but now the girl was happy because she never really had to leave a family behind — there was always a connection.

Sure!

~ THE END ~

Good-bye, cows!

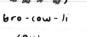 ↑
Cowmander cow
salutes you!

 ↑
bro-cow-li
cow

↑
cownstruction cow

notebook ↑
cow

Tomorrow I'm going home. I'm still figuring out what it means to have a dad. But it's O.K. if I don't have all the answers yet. At least I'm not mad at him anymore, and I know he loves me. Maybe someday I'll even learn to like Clara. For now, I'd say George is my favorite. Even if I'm not sure how to have a father, I'm already an expert on how to have a brother.

me, as a great
big sister!
↓

Maybe I have
a thing or two
to teach Cleo
about being
an older kid.

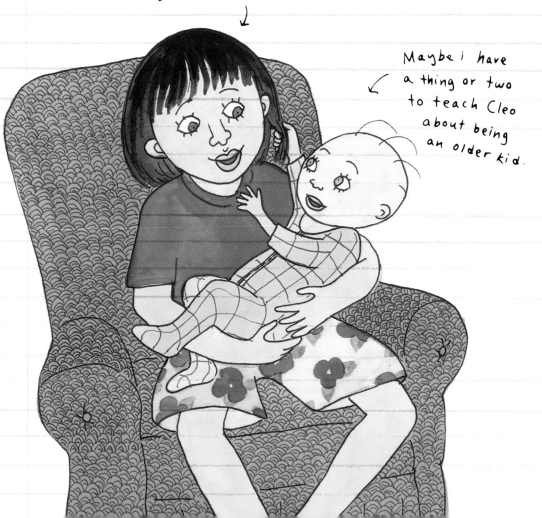